JENNY'S SHY GROOM

MAIL ORDER BRIDE OF CULVER'S CREEK

SUSANNAH CALLOWAY

Tica House Publishing

Sweet Romance that Delights and Enchants!

PERSONAL WORD FROM THE AUTHOR

Dearest Readers,

Thank you so much for choosing one of my books. I am proud to be a part of the team of writers at Tica House Publishing who work joyfully to bring you stories of hope, faith, courage, and love. Your kind words and loving readership are deeply appreciated.

I would like to personally invite you to sign up for updates and to become part of our **Exclusive Reader Club**—it's completely Free to join! We'd love to welcome you!

Much love,

Susannah Calloway

VISIT HERE to Join our Reader's Club and to Receive Tica House Updates!

https://wesrom.subscribemenow.com/

CONTENTS

CHAPTER 1

"Ouch!" Jenny yelped.

Blood dripped from Jenny's finger onto the cucumber she was slicing. It wasn't like her to be so careless, but against her better judgement, she was spending more and more time daydreaming, and that meant mistakes. She had a good position as cook for one of the best families in Boston, but it wasn't the life she craved. Her dreams took her to the open skies of Montana and the love of a good family and farm there.

"Serves you right for not paying attention," she said to herself.

Annoyed, she scraped the bloody cucumber into a trash bin and salted the cutting board. It would take her a few minutes to start over, and Mrs. Thompson, the mistress, would expect her light summer sandwiches soon. Jenny had to hurry. Fortunately, there were no distracting dreams this time, and she arranged the immaculate new cucumber sandwiches on Mrs. Thompson's hand-painted china platter. Once the food had been served, Jenny would have a moment to herself before beginning preparations for dinner.

The quiet was interrupted by a crash of plates and a young woman's gasp. Jenny knew right away who the culprit was: Lizzy the new parlor maid. The poor thing had a talent for dropping things, and it took a while to calm her down afterward. It was time to see what havoc Lizzy's latest dinner disaster had caused.

"I'm so sorry, miss. Oh, what will Mrs. Thompson say?"

The remains of hand-painted china and cucumber sandwiches lay scattered on the floor.

"I think she'll notice her favorite sandwich tray is missing, Lizzy. Now, don't start crying. I'll think of something. Unfortunately, the value will be deducted from your pay."

"But I don't have much pay left. Not after I dropped—"

"Lizzie, clean up the mess, and I'll find a new serving tray. Heaven knows Mrs. Thompson has enough of them."

Naturally, Lizzy's accident meant Jenny would have to make those sandwiches a third time. Such was the life as the cook of Boston's Thompson manor.

Of course, Mrs. Thompson had been upset that her china was in the dust bin, but at least that business was over. Lizzie was still crying hours later, but Jenny prided herself on being practical and no-nonsense, thus not much upset her. Even if her own dreams hadn't come true, for example, she prayed for strength, patience, and direction instead of giving in to despair.

After luncheon was finished and the kitchen was clean, Jenny could enjoy a few moments alone. She walked across the estate and sat in the grass. The cool grounds and the shade of her beloved tree always helped Jenny rejuvenate. But she loved this place beyond the privacy; just past the trees was a pond filled with ducks, and while their rustling and noise reminded her of the kitchen, the little birds and their ducklings made her happy.

She fanned her cheeks, flushed with summer heat, and closed her eyes. How heavenly. Her mind drifted to snow-capped mountains and fields of green. Just as she cooled down and gathered her things, she heard her name from the stables.

"Jenny! Jenny, wait for me," the voice called out.

Roy Olsen, the stable boy. Jenny debated whether to acknowledge him or pretend she hadn't heard him, but before she decided, he bounded up to her grassy perch.

"Hello Roy," she said flatly.

"Ah, Jenny, you look awful pretty today. 'Course you're always pretty."

Jenny looked over his shoulder. "Don't you have work to do? I need to go back and work in the kitchen, and I'm thinking you need to muck the stalls."

Roy didn't seem to hear her suggestion. The mere sight of her caused him to sigh like a lovesick puppy, and it annoyed Jenny to no end. He was sweet but thick in the mind. But then, Roy carried himself like a gentleman: a straw-covered, awkward, kind gentleman, she thought. Any maid would find him to be a good match, but he only had eyes for her.

She didn't share his passion. They had grown up together on the estate, and when they were young, they'd spent all their time together after the working day. Roy always looked out for her, carrying heavy loads out to the cellar or to other outbuildings until he was caught. Sometimes that got him in trouble, but he never minded. Jenny knew he'd always had feelings for her, and he was pleasant enough, but if she committed to him or anyone at the estate, her dreams of … well, of anything new and different and more exciting would be over.

Roy leaned close to her and murmured, "You're so lovely, Jenny. Do you know that? Your eyes are the deepest brown I've ever seen.

"Thank you, Roy. Truly. But I need to go…"

He touched her hand and looked her in the eyes.

"You need to open your heart, Jenny," he said. "Someday, you might find your chance of love is over, and you'll be left alone. I can't stand the thought of it. Please, give me a chance."

"Ach, Roy, you're such a romantic," said Jenny. "But I wish you would find another love – one who loves you back. You deserve that."

Jenny looked away from his much-too-familiar sad smile. There was little time to spare if she didn't get started on supper at this point, so she stood up and brushed off her skirts.

"It's good to see you, but it's time I left."

Roy tipped his hat in defeat and headed back to the stables. Jenny was sure his feelings were hurt. Perhaps it was better that way, though; she didn't want to give him ideas that would hurt him even more later.

Supper preparations for the master's family were swift and uneventful, much to Jenny's relief, and the scullery maids made quick work of the cleanup. Every copper pot, sharpened knife, and big spoon were spotless, and the hearth was swept. All perishables were stowed in the cellar, and the butter had been churned. There was nothing left to do until the next morning, at least not for Jenny. For many servants, the evening work would go on into the wee hours, but Jenny's position gave her an easier life.

It was time for the servants to eat their own supper of bread, butter, and cheese. As they all sat around the well-word table illuminated by candles, the scullery maids tittered among themselves about Lizzie's disaster. In day-to-day life, there was little amusement for the girls, so they had become gossiping experts. If one wanted to know the latest scandal, the scullery maids were the best source. Jenny was not interested, and she met each girl's gaze to remind them of their table manners.

The rest of the staff ate in silence, while others shifted their stoneware plates and mugs. Poor Lizzie sat away from the table, nibbling her bread and staring ahead with wide, watery eyes. Jenny decided it was silly to play such games with the poor parlor maid, so she broke the quiet.

"Lizzie dear, how are you doing this evening? Feeling a little better?"

Startled, the girl looked up from her bread and whispered, "Yes, thank you."

"Come, sit with us. There's room for you here."

Jenny shifted her chair to make room. After some shuffling, the nervous young girl sat beside Jenny.

"There now, you can sit with us where you belong."

The tallow candles were melting onto the table and the puddles mesmerized Lizzie and gave her something to look at besides the other maids. Jenny made a note to discuss their hurtful behavior with them the next day. In the meantime, Miss Hooper, the housekeeper, had been watching the goings-on.

"Jenny, please remember that the parlor maid and other female servants are my concern, not yours. Lizzie is fine; she just needs to watch her clumsiness, or she'll find herself on the street," said Miss Hooper.

Jenny's spine stiffened. Miss Hooper was not popular among the servants, especially those who had been in service for many years. She was a nervous older woman who had been in her position just less than a year, and she always worried about keeping up appearances and exerting her authority over her charges. More than once, she'd pinched the housemaids until they cried, usually because the grates weren't polished to a high enough sheen. Even footman Woolrich avoided the woman after she suggested he had taken the master's gold cufflinks. The cufflinks had been found soon after, but the footman was viewed with suspicion for the next few months.

All the servants and even Mr. Blake, the butler, avoided eye contact with the horrible woman. It was best to give her a wide berth as no one wanted her ire. Jenny didn't feel the same way. Human kindness was meant to be shared, and fear was an unknown to her, so as Lizzie's eyes grew wider with fright, Jenny held her hand under the table.

Jenny looked at Miss Hooper directly and said, "Yes, they are your concern. However, their well-being is everyone's concern."

If possible, the room grew even quieter. Not one servant moved or looked up from their plates. The butler, who was a kind man, looked up at Jenny just long enough to give her a little smile. Not even the scullery maids dared whisper to each other. Instead, they took tiny bites of their supper and stared at their hands.

Just then, Roy bounded in the door, looking sheepish. The young man knew how to make an appearance, Jenny thought, and his abruptness shattered the tension. The mood of the room changed, and everyone (except Miss Hooper) was happy about it. Perhaps Roy would add a different kind of excitement to the room, as he often did.

"Sorry to be late. Mr. Thompson's mare had a difficult birth, and I needed to be there for her."

"I trust you cleaned up afterward?" asked the butler.

"Course I did, that's why I'm late."

Then, Roy gave a detailed account of the birth. Unfortunately, he didn't notice the graphic description was a bit much for the maids, and even Miss Hooper's icy stare didn't deter him. With gusto, he finished, waving his hands, and nearly hollering with enthusiasm.

"The little foal had trouble with the umbilical cord wrapping around his legs, but with help, he stood on his own and gave me a little nuzzle," he practically shouted triumphantly. "It was a miracle."

Finally, the butler spoke up: "I think your descriptions are a bit too much for those not confined to the stables, Mr. Olsen. Perhaps we should observe thoughtful silence instead. It's better for the digestion."

Before long, the painful meal was over, and everyone breathed a sigh of relief.

CHAPTER 2

The wind blew softly through the swaying wheat fields, creating a river-like sound. The crops were golden, and the sun was setting over the horizon. Impossibly large mountains with snowy caps and jagged edges framed the valley and gave folks a sense of protection.

Just beyond the fields to her left, a humble cabin stood, and little children played outside. A shadowy figure of a man walked up from behind her and set his arm about her waist.

Jenny was about to say something when she awoke from her dream. It was time to start her day once again.

Jenny's day was like every other since she had taken over as cook. Shopping at the markets, preparing food, cooking the meals, and overseeing the cleanup: that was her routine. She did enjoy working in such a nice kitchen with plenty of storage, running water, and all the cookware she could want. The room even had windows that were large enough to light up the otherwise-dark room.

On the rare occasions when she had time to herself, Roy was often there. Deep down, she did care for him, but she put her affection aside because it wasn't practical. She simply wouldn't let herself be tied down, no matter how sweet he was.

Roy wasn't the only young man to show an interest in her. In fact, several of the servants and even the butler had noticed her. That fact mostly escaped Jenny because she had no idea how beautiful she was. While she always tried to make herself "presentable," the concept of vanity didn't sit well with her no-nonsense personality.

Just as every other day, Jenny started the morning by going to the markets. Rather than carrying the load on her own, Jenny always had Mildred, the under cook, come with her.

"Mildred, time to leave."

"Just a moment, miss."

"What is taking so long?"

Jenny did her best to be patient, but she gathered her things, opened the servants' outside door, and tapped her foot.

"Are you gossiping again? Mildred, it's time to leave."

After some shuffling and giggling noises, Mildred turned the corner, ready to go. Then, the two women began the hour walk. While the early-morning trip was time consuming, it gave Jenny a chance to leave the house and walk unfettered through the meadows. It didn't take long for her thoughts to wander off into wheat fields and mountains. Unfortunately, her musings were interrupted.

"Oh miss, aren't them wildflowers pretty?" cried Mildred.

Jenny sighed, "Yes, yes they are."

"Do you think I could gather a few? They make my room prettier."

"They'd die before we got back."

Mildred scowled in frustration. "Well, maybe on the way back?"

Jenny sighed again. "Of course, but I still say they won't last."

The sun's heat created a bead of sweat on her brow. Maybe it was the heat, or maybe it was her secret dream invading her thoughts again, but Jenny couldn't take it anymore. Though Jenny didn't show her feelings to Mildred, she prayed silently for help. There must be a way to escape the same tasks every day. There must be a way to find that field in the mountains. She rested in her faith that all would work out as it should. But sometimes, it was just plain harder to believe.

~

The market was bustling with servants and locals alike, and all were looking for the best bargains. Chickens and geese squawked in their cages while the vendors' voices rose above the fray. Each stall sold a different type of merchandise, from fruits and vegetables to meat and cheese. When Jenny was little, it seemed like a massive collection of wonders, but as an adult, she thought only of collecting items for the day's meals.

Jenny had her own route, and she always began with her favorite vegetable seller, Amelia. As she grew close to the woman's stall, she saw no sign of the vendor. In her place stood a young girl.

"What can I get ya?" asked the girl.

"Where's Amelia?" Jenny asked.

The girl pushed a stray blond hair back, only to have it fall forward again. "Gone," she said and tilted her head like a bird to look at Jenny with interest.

"What do you mean? Gone where?"

"On her way to Montana."

"What? Why? Is she all right?"

The girl seemed unfazed by Jenny's concern. "She answered one of them adverts for a Mail Order Bride. So excited, that one. Couldn't wait to leave. Said it was the adventure of a lifetime." The girl cocked her head again and asked, "Is something bothering you?"

Jenny was taken aback. The girl was certainly direct, and while Jenny appreciated it, no one in the market usually asked her a personal question like that. Ordinarily, Jenny wouldn't confide in anyone, let alone a stranger, but for some reason she felt compelled to respond. She sent Mildred off to look for cherries. The under cook seemed blissfully unaware, but Jenny didn't want anyone on staff to know her thoughts.

"You don't look so happy," said the girl.

"I'm happy enough."

"Hmm… all right. I still think something's bothering you, and I'm good at noticing things."

"I work for the Thompson family, and it's a good position."

"But?"

Jenny took a deep breath and then blurted, "But I can't shake the feeling that I'm meant to be somewhere else and doing something else."

The girl stood with her hand on her right cheek. It was obvious she was pondering Jenny's words. Jenny relayed her dream of farming out West with a family beside her to share the adventure. It felt good to finally share her dream with someone—even though that someone was a stranger.

The girl grinned and asked, "What do you think of Mail Order Brides?"

CHAPTER 3

"And what exactly is a Mail Order Bride?" asked Jenny. "It sounds like something unnatural."

"Oh no, it's good for a new start."

"How does it work?" she asked.

"There's a newspaper called *Matrimonial Times* that helps women here and men out west find each other. Happens all the time, people just don't talk about it in Boston. Just look through the adverts 'til ya find a good one. That's what Amelia did."

"Just like that?"

"Well, most folks write each other a few times first."

Jenny wasn't sure what to think, but she didn't dismiss the idea out of hand. She gathered the vegetables for that day's menu and thanked the girl for her advice. They had just finished talking when Mildred wandered back with a basket of bruised cherries. Why did Jenny think the girl was reliable?

"By the way, I'm Harriet," said the girl. "And your name is?"

"Jenny, and thanks." She turned and started off to visit other vendors.

"See you again soon," Harriet called out after them.

By the time Jenny and Mildred reached the kitchen, Jenny had a headache. It felt like a hailstorm was pouring over the back of her head. Mildred was happy with her wilted wildflowers, but Jenny was once again lost in thought.

Had the Lord sent Harriet to her, or was it too good to be true? What kind of person placed an advertisement for marriage? She'd have to think about it before jumping in with both feet. After all, that was the practical thing to do.

"Something smells good."

"Hello, Roy. Why are you in the kitchen?" Jenny asked.

Roy had a silly grin on his face and a twinkle in his eye.

She scrutinized him. "What're you up to? And why the smile? Have some good news?"

"I did it. I did it, Jenny. I got the leg-up. You're looking at the new stable master."

Jenny clapped her hands and smiled. "Congratulations. How'd that happen?"

Roy wrinkled his nose with faux distain.

"What, didn't think I had it in me? The old man's retiring, and he thought I was the best one to fill his shoes. Said I was great with the birth last night, and he'd like to see me stay on."

Jenny laughed with pleasure. Though she didn't want to give him any ideas, she was still proud of him.

"Are you happy? Are you proud of me?"

"Well, of course, I am. You deserve the best," she said. "Here, have some coffee. I can't sit around with you, of course…"

"Got to get back at work, but thanks, Jenny. I knew you cared."

Jenny watched through the window as he crossed the lawn, and she couldn't help but smile widely. He was a good fellow.

The day passed into night, and it was time for Jenny to head up to her room. She lived in the servant's quarters with the others, but she had one of the better rooms, and it was all due to the lady of the manor. Mrs. Thompson always did like Jenny, even when Jenny was just a scullery maid. Perhaps it was her excellent work, or maybe it was her devotion to learning new things, but Mrs. Thompson was happy to hire her on as cook when the position opened.

Jenny's room was spare of furnishings, but what she did have were hand-me-downs from Mrs. Thompson herself. The chair next to Jenny's bed had been in the parlor for two generations, but now it was hers. While the upholstery was faded and worn, Jenny loved to sit in it and look out her small window overlooking the formal gardens.

As usual, she spent the last hours of her day sitting in her chair, reading her Bible, and talking to the good Lord. There were so many things to be thankful for, but one prayer was still left unanswered.

"Please help me get to Montana," she whispered. For she was sure that faraway Montana had the mountain and the fields she dreamed about.

The next day, Jenny decided to contact Harriet again and look into this "Mail Order Bride business." She was about to leave for the market when Roy met her at the door.

"Hello, Jenny. You look pretty today."

"You say that every day."

"Because it's true. You're lovely," he said, "and it seems a shame not to remind you. Besides, I love your smooth skin and chestnut curls." Roy paused. "Say, isn't it a little early for the market? Everything all right?"

Jenny smiled, but her face turned crimson with embarrassment. Roy looked surprised and backed away from the door to allow her passage.

"Did I say something wrong? Oh, I'm an oaf, barging in like that. I'll head back out to the stables. Really should be out there now, taking care of the new foal."

"No, Roy, it's fine. I just thought leaving early would mean missing the heat. Though on second thought, maybe I should send Mildred out on her own. It's too hot for me, and she doesn't mind. Really, don't worry about it." Jenny was backtracking now, not wanting Roy to find out the reason for her early departure.

Roy's shoulders relaxed.

"Long as I'm not bothering you. The last thing I want to be is a pest."

She gave him a slight smile. "Well, not always," she said, and they laughed.

~

"Alone?" asked Mildred.

"Yes. It'll be good for you. Remember what I taught you about haggling and finding the best price. And no bruised fruit this time, all right?"

"I… I suppose. I'll do my best, Miss," she said.

As Mildred nodded her head and gathered her things. Jenny wondered if she had made the right decision in changing her plans so suddenly. Surely, no one would be suspicious simply because she was leaving early. Still, it was done now. She could meet with Harriet another day.

Since Jenny had a few extra moments to herself, she headed for her favorite grassy knoll and sat down. The cool grass and the shade of her beloved tree once again helped to calm her. The little ducklings waddling about the pond had grown in just the past day, and they were flapping their newly feathered wings. Jenny forgot her troubles for a moment and just watched.

Her thoughts returned to that morning. Jenny forgave Roy for prying because he had no idea she was hiding a secret. Still, the thought of being caught before anything was arranged frightened her. She would lose her position and have nowhere to go. Young unmarried ladies with no income were vulnerable to starving and living in the streets, and in truth, the thought made Jenny squirm.

Having a chance to collect her thoughts was very helpful, even more than her usual afternoon moments. She loved her solitude if no one bothered her there. Unfortunately, Roy had a habit of interrupting her peace. Most of the time, she endured it because he was such a dear, but there were other times when she wasn't so patient. Today was one of those days.

Here he came, flowers in hand. He was covered in pieces of hay, and his boots were caked in muck. That didn't seem to bother him, however. Even when he was a child, he enjoyed playing in the dirt and would make mud pies with Jenny (until she learned that being dirty was frowned upon by kitchen staff).

"I know I shouldn't stay, but these flowers reminded me of you. I felt bad about this morning, and these are for you."

"Thank you," she said, wishing he hadn't come. "The flowers are lovely... Goodness, but you remind me of Mildred. Always picking wildflowers only to have them half die on the way home. How did you have a spare moment, anyway? Why aren't you at the stable?"

Roy was crestfallen and let the flowers fall in a sad lump on the ground. "Them flowers might be a bit wilted, but... I love you, Jenny. It's no secret."

Jenny's breath caught. Why couldn't she return his love? It would be so much simpler if she could. "I know, Roy, but—"

Roy interrupted her. "I want you to marry me. I have a good position now, and I could support you. I might not yet have money for a ring, but…"

She sucked in her breath. "No, Roy, I can't marry you. I can't marry anyone here. Surely you know that. Have I ever said I loved you?"

"Not in so many words." He looked so crestfallen, that her chest tightened. This was awful.

"I'm sorry, Roy. Truly, I am."

"No. It's me who's sorry. I-I'm a fool. I won't bother you again."

He walked back to the stable, his head down and shoulders stooped. Jenny knew she had broken his heart. Roy had always been a sensitive and stubborn soul, and how she wished she could have returned his declaration of love. She worried she had been impatient with him and wondered if there was anything she could say later that might soothe his feelings.

It wasn't the first time Jenny's temper got her in trouble. As a teenager, she'd hollered at a fellow scullery maid for not cleaning the fish for the master's party that night, and the girl had burst into tears. Jenny felt vindicated, at least at first; that was until the cook told her the girl would get hives every time she touched fish.

"A scabbed over, suffering scullery maid is no use to me," said the cook, "You focus on your own duties and leave the overseeing to me."

Jenny remembered that lesson, and as she grew older, it was easier to suppress her temper, but not always.

Roy was missing from the servant's supper that night. No one said a word, and the silence was oppressive to Jenny. It was obvious her rejection of Roy's proposal was common knowledge now, even though no one mentioned it.

Even the scullery maids weren't talking; they simply ate in silence and stared at Jenny when they thought she wasn't looking. Finally, Jenny pushed her bread and cheese aside. The tension was too much to bear, so she excused herself and headed out to the stables. On her way out the door, she heard the young maids start right in gossiping about her.

Jenny stood by the big, wooden stable door and watched Roy. He stood alone in a stall with the young foal and its mother. He was brushing the mare, but not with much heart this time. The animal nuzzled his arm, and he stroked her face. It had been a very long day for everyone, and Jenny knew it.

Whenever Roy was troubled, Jenny knew horses lifted his spirits, but not even the mare and her baby seemed enough for him this time. Jenny watched him for a while. She felt terrible, not for turning him down, but for the pain she'd caused.

Just then, she sneezed. Roy whirled around.

"Jenny, I'm surprised to see you here," he said and turned back to the mare.

"Roy, I need to let you know—"

"I understand. You don't love me and never did. Even as children, when I gave you flowers, you wouldn't take them. You'd say they were happier living in the ground. I was a fool not to see my love was one-sided, even when you gave me hints all along."

"Let me finish, Roy. I was going to say I'm sorry for the way things turned out. While it's true I don't want to marry you, I do have feelings for you. They just aren't … romantic."

He stopped brushing the horse and looked over at her.

"I don't need pity. I'm a grown man who should know when to stop pursuing."

"I'm so sorry, Roy. I'm sorry I hurt you, but I had to be forthcoming."

"I understand. You are a grown woman who knows what she does and doesn't want. It's good you didn't accept my proposal if you don't … love me. It's just going to take a while for me to feel better." He paused. "Shouldn't you be at supper?"

"Shouldn't you?" she replied. "It isn't good for you to skip a meal."

"So now you're worried about me?" Roy smiled sadly.

"Of course, I am. I care about you a great deal, and I want you to come back to the manor with me."

After some coaxing, Roy left the horses, and they walked back to the servant's entrance to finish their meal. The other servants had left, and the dishes had been washed, so Jenny brought out some fresh bread and cheese. Roy bowed his head for silent grace, and the two ate together. Then they went to their rooms for the night. It had been a long day indeed.

CHAPTER 4

Morning came as it always does, and Jenny faced the day with a mixture of trepidation and excitement. It was a strange combination, and it left her stomach unsettled. On one hand, she was worried about Roy. On the other, she was determined more than ever to pursue her dreams. She was going to become a Mail Order Bride.

But how? Jenny decided to seek out Harriet, the young vegetable seller, for more information. There was a need for more onions for the night's meal, so going to the market for a special trip wouldn't raise suspicion. As she headed out the door and into the fresh air, she couldn't help but miss Roy's frequent interruption, which surprised her greatly.

Thankfully, the young girl was there at the vegetable stall, but this time, others were buying vegetables at the stand. Jenny was patient; she couldn't afford the gossip, of course, so she stood aside. Half an hour passed before she saw an opening.

Harriet looked up from her last transaction and nodded to Jenny.

"I see you're back. Given it any thought? Want to be a Mail Order Bride or are you just interested in the vegetables today?" asked Harriet.

Jenny was mortified. "Please talk more quietly. And yes, I'm interested. How do I start? I need to keep this quiet for now."

"Don't want anyone to know? All right. I kept a copy of *Matrimonial Times* with me in case you came back. I told you, I've got a nose for these things."

Harriet gave her the copy. "There. People will only think you bought a paper."

Jenny nodded and headed back to the manor, clutching her prize in one hand and a braid of onions in the other.

After stowing the newspaper under her thin mattress, Jenny made her way to the kitchen. This day couldn't go by fast enough. She went through her tasks: preparing, cooking, and supervising. Of course, the scullery maids were still whispering about the scandal surrounding Roy's proposal, but Jenny wasn't interested anymore in their titter. Instead, she focused her thoughts on what she wanted in a husband and a new life. Since there would be so many posts from lonely farmers, it would help to narrow the search.

After some thought, she settled on a young man in his twenties, a man with good moral character, and a man of decent means. Deep down, she also hoped to find love, but she set that thought aside. There would be time to worry about that later; for now, she'd pray for guidance. In the meantime, there was a pheasant to cook.

Finally, after the day was through, Jenny was alone in her room. It was time to take the first step. What would she find? Her pulse throbbed in her temples as she opened the paper. Could this be her destiny? Would she be a woman of the Wild West?

After searching for some time, her excitement waned. Most advertisements were so short, it was impossible to know much about any of the bachelors. She was about to give up with she saw this post:

Matrimonial – Gentleman, aged 26, Christian, hardworking, and educated. Looking for a

good woman willing to live and work on a farm in Montana.

Could this be the one? It was so hard to tell, but correspondence would help. Dare she try? Dare she take the first step? Jenny's hands began to shake.

That night, she fell asleep mid-prayer, sitting in her chair by the bed.

Wind blew softly through the swaying wheat fields, creating a river-like sound. The crops were golden, ready to harvest, and the sun was setting over the horizon. Impossibly large mountains with snowy caps and jagged edges framed the valley and gave her a sense that all was well.

Just beyond the fields to her left, a humble cabin stood, and little children were playing outside. The cabin was small but tidy, and a pot of flowers sat cheerfully by the door. A shadowy figure of a man walked up from behind her and set his arm around her waist. When Jenny tried to say something, the man, the children, and the fields all disappeared.

It was morning again.

Jenny had experienced that dream many times, and each time it was more difficult to let go and wake up. She knew in her heart she was meant to be there, and with some grace, she would be. Stiff from sleeping in an awkward position, Jenny stood and stretched. She looked down at the wrinkled copy of *Matrimonial Times* and wondered if it really did hold the key to her future. Perhaps, but for now, it was time to head down to the kitchen. She slid the paper under her mattress again and started her day.

The day had been surprisingly uneventful aside from calming Lizzie after she broke a teacup. The problem with peaceful days was how they dragged on. Still, Jenny went through the motions of her duties and tried to act normally.

After Jenny praised Mildred a third time for keeping the scullery maids busy, Mildred said, "Miss, is everything all right?"

Jenny looked startled.

"Of course, everything's fine. Be on your way then, and thank you..."

"Thank you for what? Keeping them scullery maids in line? Yes, miss. You're welcome... again," said Mildred as she eyed Jenny with suspicion.

The other maids looked up in interest and whispered to each other. When Jenny caught their eyes, the girls went back to work as if nothing had happened. Acting "normally" wasn't going the way she planned.

It seemed like an eternity passed before Jenny entered her private chamber that night. She sat at her carved desk and began to write. The desk was a wonderful mahogany with cherubs carved in the feet, and while it too was a hand-me-down gift from Mrs. Thompson, and Jenny was grateful, she always felt a little uncomfortable when using it. Did she really merit such a nice (albeit worn) piece of furniture?

She set aside her discomfort and penned a quick letter.

Dear Sir,

I am a young Christian woman, 20, and not afraid of hard work. I have a very practical

nature and appreciate good sense. Please respond if interested.

There it was – her key to possible freedom. The letter was brief, but it made sense to keep it that way. For all she knew, the man had already met his bride.

Jenny went to bed and slept fitfully, dreaming about Montana, for the rest of the night.

CHAPTER 5

The next morning, Jenny greeted the sun with a smile. While her stomach was still upset by nerves, her heart was light. As she headed to the market with Mildred that day, Jenny decided she would send the letter off with Harriet. Surely Harriet would help; it had been her idea, after all.

Jenny sent Mildred on an errand and hurried over to Harriet.

"You seem excited," said Harriet. "Did you find a good match or two?"

As usual, the placid girl was unfazed by any excitement. She stood on one foot and scratched her leg with her other.

"I'm just sending out one letter for now. I want to see how it goes," said Jenny.

"Don't wait too long; them bachelors often find a bride quickly. Have you sent it yet?"

"There's an issue…"

"You don't want the other servants to see, or they'll ruin your plans. Is that it? You want me to post it?"

Jenny let out a sigh of relief.

"Would you? I have the postage here."

The girl nodded and took Jenny's letter. She jostled the letter in her hand and cocked her head: "Awfully light. Miss Brown would send longer letters. Her bachelor got to know her quicker that way. You sure you want to send this out?"

Jenny knew Harriet was probably right, but she didn't change her mind.

"Yes, I'm sure."

It was time to go, but Mildred was distracted by the wildflowers, picking some unfortunate blooms to wilt in her hand. Jenny watched her thoughtfully. Maybe Roy was onto something: enjoy life before it's too late. Mildred sure did seem to be enjoying the flowers.

That night, Jenny prayed about the letter and the man she'd sent it to. It was in the Lord's hands now.

There was one wrinkle in Jenny's plan, and that was incoming mail. Mr. Blake, the butler, collected all incoming correspondence, sorted the pile for each recipient, and carried the pile on a silver tray to the appropriate room. Servant's letters would be carried separately, though there were precious few. They were often opened and reviewed as a matter of course, so Jenny had to come up with a plan.

For two weeks, Jenny had a new morning routine while waiting for a reply. From a hiding spot in the parlor behind Mrs. Thompson's favorite floor vase, Jenny watched for the mail. It came at the same time of day, and Mr. Blake would arrive ten to fifteen minutes after. That left a small window of time for Jenny to sort through the letters to look for her own. She also had to contend with the other servants bustling around, cleaning and straightening everything. It was a delicate dance, but she managed to complete it each day.

Her habit wasn't as secret as she had hoped, for Mildred grew curious and followed her to the parlor one day. Just as Jenny started leafing through the letters, Mildred startled her.

"Miss? What're you doing?" she whispered, "Do you want to be turned out onto the streets? No one would hire you after, you know."

Jenny jumped so high with fright that a few strands of hair came loose from where she'd tucked them behind her ears. It would have been funny, had it not been so serious. After a few seconds, Jenny gathered her wits.

"Well, I suppose there's no hiding it from you now. I'm waiting for a letter."

"Who from?"

"I can't say, but it's coming from Montana."

"Is it Amelia, the vegetable seller? Didn't she go there?"

Suddenly, a light went on for Jenny. Amelia. She could be the go-between. Jenny wondered if Amelia and her own potential husband were close to each other in Montana. The truth was, she had no idea how large the state was, but the thought gave her hope. Why hadn't she thought of that before?

"Miss? Miss, if we don't hurry, Mr. Blake will be here and demand to know what's going on. Come now, hurry."

Jenny looked through the rest of the letter pile before turning to go. She gave a start, hardly believing her good fortune. There was the letter she'd been waiting for. She slipped it into her bodice and followed Mildred back to the kitchen. Jenny knew Mildred would ask more questions, but for now, all was well. At least, it seemed that way.

All day long, Jenny moved about carefully. None of the servants could hear the letter crinkling under her bodice, or at least she hoped so. She focused on preparing the day's meals, but the scullery maids could tell she was on edge. Worse yet, Mildred knew something was up too.

"Miss?"

Jenny jumped straight up and stiffened her spine.

"Yes Mildred? What is it?" she asked. Her hands were trembling so much that she dropped her knife.

"Are you all right? You seem right spooked. And then there's them letters…"

"I'm fine. Please don't speak of our adventure this morning. Now, what is it?"

"We need more fennel. Should I go fetch some from the market?"

"Of all the… yes, Mildred. Go, and hurry. The master and mistress will expect dinner soon."

"Yes, miss."

As the girl scampered out the door, Jenny turned back to her work. She stirred a pot of Mrs. Thompson's favorite soup and looked over to the pile of vegetables for tonight's dinner. To her surprise, there was the fennel, right where it should have been. She frowned. That silly girl hadn't been paying attention. Oh, this day couldn't be over soon enough.

Jenny opened the letter in the low lamplight of her room. The writing was neat, and the content was sparse, but she still felt her heart flutter as she read.

Dear Jenny,

I am glad to hear from you, but I have some news. I have already met and married my bride. I am sorry; perhaps it was not meant to be. Do not give up hope. There are many of us out here, looking for a good wife.

Sincerely,

Joe Harper

Jenny let the letter fall from her hand to the floor and wept. All the stress hadn't been

worth it. Perhaps she should marry Roy if he'd still have her. Maybe her dream was too far-fetched. She folded the letter and stashed it under her mattress. It was time to pray and go to sleep.

Wind blew softly through the swaying wheat fields, creating a river-like sound. The crops were golden, ready to reap, and the sun was setting over the horizon. Impossibly large mountains with

snowy caps and jagged edges framed the valley and gave her a sense of protection. The trees, just beyond reaches of their farm, whispered as the wind blew through their boughs.

Just beyond the fields to her left, a humble cabin stood. It was small but tidy, and a pot of flowers sat cheerfully by the door. Little children were laughing as they played and ran in circles after each other. A shadowy figure of a man walked up from behind her and set his arm around her waist. She could almost make out his face, and somehow, she knew he was handsome. When the man tried to say something, he, the children, the cabin, and the fields all disappeared.

It was time to get up.

CHAPTER 6

What would today bring? Jenny didn't want to face it, that was for sure. The rejection hit her hard, and it would take a while to heal. Suddenly, she understood Roy's reaction to her dismissal. It hurt. But maybe there was another way for her to go. Maybe her friend Amelia could help.

When at the market later that morning, Jenny approached Harriet. The girl was counting coins while chewing on her lip.

"Hello, Harriet. I see you're busy. Maybe later?" Jenny asked.

The girl kept counting and then paused. "Don't mind me. What do you need, and where's Mildred? Did you send her away again? The girl's bound to get suspicious. She came by yesterday, saying she needed fennel. If you ask me, she was tryin' to pry. Asked me all kinds of strange questions."

"Did you say anything?" Jenny gasped.

"Course not. I wouldn't help someone only to turn on them. Now, what do ya need?"

"Do you have Amelia's address? I've given up on *Matrimonial Times.*"

Harriet looked up from her coins and squinted her eyes.

"You sure? Didn't you just try once? Gonna take more tries than that."

"Yes, I'm sure. I'm starting to feel a bit desperate. And Mildred is suspicious. She caught me waiting for a letter a few days ago, and I had to think on my feet."

"Well, it just so happens I do have Amelia's address. She wanted to keep in touch with Boston and the people she knew here. Very sentimental, that one."

"Sounds like her. Could I have it? Before Mildred comes back?"

"Too late, she's here," said Harriet.

"Hello, miss. I got the things you asked for. This time, no bruises on the fruit."

Jenny feigned a laugh and said, "It sounds like you do have some good sense. Hurry, let's get back home. You go on ahead of me. I'll be right behind you."

Mildred stood her ground.

"Miss, what's going on? Is something wrong?"

"My goodness no. Just go please. Find some wildflowers to pick."

The girl turned reluctantly and headed out to the meadow. Mildred might not be the smartest girl she'd ever known, but she was stubborn, and if she found out Jenny was hoping to leave her post, she could be dismissed quickly.

Harriet whispered, "Here. Now go and good luck."

By the time they reached the kitchen, both Jenny and Mildred were quiet. In fact, neither had said a word since they left the market. Jenny was upset with herself for getting into this mess in the first place. She'd always prided herself on being practical, and this adventure was anything but. She prayed silently for guidance and patience until she and Mildred parted to do their separate chores.

When Jenny felt overwhelmed, she would try to form a plan, so when her few daily moments of solitude arrived, she headed to her favorite spot in the grass by the pond and thought things through. The air was so still Jenny could hear her own breathing. No ducklings were to be found, and Roy was over at the stable. As she waited for the usual calm that descended upon her there, she was restless. On impulse, she jumped up. Goodness, but she needed to get ahold of herself.

~

Roy was already on his way to the servant's dining room. At supper, once everyone began eating, Roy thoroughly described a mare's "intestinal issues," much to everyone's dismay except Jenny's. She stifled a laugh as Mrs. Hooper turned green and pushed away her plate.

"Really, Roy, you are the most inappropriate boy I've ever known. Look, you've spoiled our appetites. Poor Mildred's sick and hiding it behind her napkin. Mr. Blake, control your man."

The butler collected himself and looked over at Mrs. Hooper.

"No, Mildred isn't sick. She's laughing. If you haven't noticed by now, Roy loves to tease you with the least palatable stories he can find from the stables. Perhaps if you didn't react so strongly, he would be less forthcoming with so many details."

Mrs. Hooper stood up so suddenly that she shook the table, and Jenny's mug of milk teetered.

"This is outrageous," she sputtered.

She huffed out the door and up the servant's stairs to her room. Once she was gone, Mr. Blake pulled Roy aside. Jenny couldn't hear their conversation over the excited whispers of the other servants, but she hoped Roy wouldn't be in too much trouble. He was a rascal sometimes, but that was part of his charm.

Sometime later, the two men emerged and sat down. Roy looked serious but not upset, so Jenny breathed a little easier.

Mildred laughed. "Roy, what would we do without you? The miss may not want you, but we do. Every time Mrs. Hooper is unbearable, you make her go away. You…"

Jenny shot a glance to her under cook. "Mildred, be careful. Goodness, but what a day. I think it's my turn to go upstairs. Good night."

Roy touched her arm as she passed, and while she didn't react, she felt some comfort.

When Jenny reached her room, she sat at the edge of her bed and prayed. She prayed for herself, but she prayed for Roy, too. And then she got down to business.

A blank page sat intimidatingly on the desk. For what seemed like an hour, Jenny stared at it. Finally, she moved over to her chair and looked out the window onto the beautiful dimming landscape. The shrubs were trimmed into swirls of green and the paths between were white with tiny, smooth pebbles. At the center was a marble fountain that never stopped flowing until the dead of winter. Jenny loved staring at the water as it cascaded down the statue of a lady holding a vase.

Jenny felt a sense of calm and walked back to her desk and began to write.

Dear Amelia,

How are you, my dear friend? I have missed you at the vegetable market. How is Montana? Harriet told me you were a Mail Order Bride, and I thought about following that same path. Did it work well for you? If so, do you know of any suitable bachelors who would take an interest? I'm sorry to ask so many questions, but as you know, I've always wanted a way out of service. I can only imagine what it's like to live free, and I hope it's what I dreamed. Please respond as soon as you can.

Your friend,

Jenny

CHAPTER 7

Amelia sat in her rocking chair, repairing stockings. Her husband, Joseph Spencer, went through them so fast. Still, she didn't begrudge him. After all, he worked hard and long. She hummed a song from her childhood as she sewed and rocked herself until she was sleepy. Her husband was already in bed, for mornings came all too early. Amelia didn't stay up much later than he, but she enjoyed a little quiet time to think.

She'd been in Montana for three months, and it had been nearly all she had hoped. Joseph was kind, the house was small but comfortable, and the food was plentiful. She worked from before the sun rose to after it set, but it was a good life.

Another aspect of life with Joseph was his children. Joseph had been married before, but his first wife had died giving birth to their second child, Ruby. Their oldest, Bartholomew, was devoted to Ruby and watched over her with care, while Ruby giggled and played with the wooden doll Joseph had carved for her. The children were still young – Bartholomew was six and Ruby was four – so Amelia had an easy time getting to know them.

Bartholomew had dark brown hair, just like his father, and he loved to be silly. Quite often, he would chase the chickens around the coop when he was supposed to be gathering the eggs. Rather than getting angry, however, Amelia taught him to make friends with them. At first, he wasn't convinced, but when Ruby toddled in and started petting the littlest hen of the bunch, he went along with it.

By contrast, Ruby was a serious child who loved animals. She would talk to the pigs, goats, and chickens, and while they didn't know what she was saying, they were still good listeners. She could spend hours outside, prattling away.

While sometimes the two of them were a handful, Amelia found herself "loving them to pieces" almost right away. Truly, the only drawback of this life was a lack of female friends. Not many women would take the journey she did to face the unknown, and she was one of few women around.

She and her husband did have friends from other homesteads nearer town. Culver's Creek was humble, but the people were honest and good; at least Amelia thought so. Everyone went to church together on Sundays, and she often put together a big meal for the parishioners in the afternoon. While it was good work that made the men happy, it would have been nice for her to have a female friend, one that could help in the kitchen and watch the children with her. Amelia also thought it would be nice to talk about something other than crops and weather. She was a city girl, after all.

The next day, a letter arrived from Boston for Amelia. Shaking from excitement, she tore the envelope, tossed it to the ground, and started to read. It was from her old market friend, Jenny. As Amelia read, her eyes grew wider and wider. Jenny wanted to come here and settle down. Was it too good to be true?

By the end of the letter, tears rolled down Amelia's thin, pink cheeks. There were bachelor farmers here looking for a wife, so it wouldn't be too difficult. And not just anyone, but her dear friend would come to live here. Amelia realized she might be getting ahead of herself, however. First, she had to find the right bachelor for Jenny.

Joseph was already out in the fields with the farm hands, and the children were doing their chores, so Amelia kept the news to herself. While she prepared dinner for the workers, she sifted through the list of eligible bachelors in her mind.

There was Henry Stiller, but he was too emotional and hot-tempered for her friend. That wouldn't do. She eliminated a couple more from the list in her head before she landed on the right one: Robert Davenport.

Robert was handsome, reliable, and practical. He wasn't a talkative man, but he had a reputation for honesty and hard work. He might not have had the biggest farm in the area, but it was successful. That meant Jenny would live in comfort with a decent husband if he consented. In the meantime, she must think of what to say. How would she describe her friend to him?

The farmers didn't gather until Sundays or special events, so it would have to wait. Today was Friday, and it would give her time to think of how to approach Robert. In the meantime, Amelia's day was filled with cooking, washing linens, and tending their personal garden with the children. Keeping the dust out of their home was a nonstop chore as well. So, when Joseph came in with the farmhands for dinner, Amelia couldn't wait to tell him the news.

Once everyone was seated and just before grace, Amelia blurted out, "Joseph, what if I told you there's a new lady coming to town?"

He raised an eyebrow.

"Where did ya hear that? Not much gossip 'round here, and if there was, I'd know."

"I received a letter from a dear friend today. She wants to come here and find a husband. I know just the bachelor, too."

There was a twinkle in his eye as he asked, "Do you? Have you spoken to this mystery gentleman yet?"

"Not yet, but I hope to this Sunday. I'm thinking of Robert Davenport. Wouldn't he be perfect?" Amelia likely shouldn't be sharing this with all the hands present, but she was simply too excited to wait.

"Robert's a good man."

"He is, and Jenny's just right. She's practical and hard-working, just like he is."

The farmhands looked hungry, and the children were squirming. Dinner couldn't wait much longer for them, so Joseph put an end to the conversation by adding, "You might wanna ask him first 'fore marrying him off."

Amelia's pink cheeks flushed red. She knew he was right, of course, but she was beyond excited to have a friend close by.

"I'll take her," one of the hands said.

"So will I," another said, and all the men started guffawing and claiming the new woman.

"I'm sorry, men," Amelia said. "But I've got it all planned out."

After many groans, grace was said, and everyone tucked in. The men talked about the weather and the condition of the crops. It was an all-too-familiar conversation for Amelia of course, but that night, she didn't mind; she was distracted. She was planning social and work activities she could share with Jenny, and light suppers with the happy couple on Saturday nights. All the while, she shuffled food from one side of her plate to the other and gazed out the window at the fields that stretched out for miles. Sunday couldn't come soon enough.

Robert Davenport looked up at the sky. It was a peaceful, sunny Saturday, except for the fact he was flat on his back, and his horse, Angus, was stomping the ground beside him with gusto. Oh, how his horse hated snakes. It wasn't always the case; the first time Angus saw one, he was curious. That curiosity earned him an encounter that he barely survived. Luckily, Robert was an expert horseman and knew what to do. Now, whenever the horse saw a snake, he would pulverize the critter with his hoof.

Robert assumed it was revenge, but whatever the reason, it sometimes meant being thrown to the ground. Today was one of those days. Robert stood up, brushed himself off, and grabbed the reins of his horse.

"Come on, Angus. Don't think that critter is gonna bother you now."

The sun was setting behind the snow-capped mountains as Robert and Angus reached the barn. The rays of pink sunlight meant a late supper and an early bedtime, both for him and his horse. He led Angus to his stall, gave the horse a good brushing, and then headed to his own little cabin.

After a dinner of beans, Robert nursed his bruised hip. Life was pretty good, he thought. His fields were fertile, his animals were healthy, and his belly was full. What else was there in life? Some companionship might be nice. After a little contemplation, he limped off to bed and slept well.

CHAPTER 8

It was a Sunday, and everyone was in their seats, waiting for the reverend. Amelia sat at the foot-pump organ and looked for the sign to start. Eventually, the elderly minister shuffled into view and nodded; it was time for hymns and thanksgiving. While it was true that Amelia wasn't a very talented organist, she was enthusiastic. Most of the congregation had better sense than to wince when she hit a clunker, and fortunately, the painful mistakes were fewer and fewer the longer she played.

Reverend Johnson spoke about the love and grace of God. He might have been old, but he could still speak with authority. His rumbling voice could fill the pews and keep even the sleepiest parishioner awake. His eyes weren't what they used to be, and it was difficult for him to read the fine print of his Bible, but it didn't matter too much – he'd memorized many scriptures years ago. After the last hymn, he walked up to each man there and shook his hand.

With everyone milling around after the service, Amelia hurried to finish preparations for the big dinner. It was a lot of work, and the thought of having more help made her happy. Little Ruby was a dear and loved to help, but she usually made a bigger mess, while Bartholomew would invariably wander off to make some mischief.

Jenny was an excellent cook and would hopefully teach her a thing or two about organizing meals and getting things just right. She might even help with the children, and Amelia knew her friend would likely be much stricter than she was. Perhaps that would be a good thing, at least when it came to the boy. Once the meal was ready, she saw Robert pass by, but couldn't get his attention.

When Joseph headed to their usual bench for dinner, Amelia caught his arm.

"Please, could we sit over there?" she asked.

"This wouldn't have anything to do with your matchmaking, would it?"

"Please, Joseph, this is important."

He smiled and patted her hand.

"Of course, my dear. Let's see if the Ellsworth brothers will switch places with us."

It took some coaxing, as the brothers were rather set in their ways, but Amelia had her seat next to Robert. He wasn't much of a talker, so she started the conversation.

"Hello Robert. How are you this fine Sunday? I saw you were walking with a limp. Is everything all right?"

Robert looked up from his plate.

He seemed confused at her barrage, so she started over: "How are you today? How's your leg?"

"Leg's okay, I guess. Got thrown off my horse yesterday."

He said nothing more and began to eat. This wasn't going the way Amelia had planned, so she squeezed her husband's arm as a plea for help.

Joseph didn't like awkward silence, so he added,

"Robert, got any new ideas on where to take our harvests this fall? It's just two months away, you know."

Robert perked up, and they began a lengthy conversation about wheat and the best way to use manure as a fertilizer. Amelia's thoughts would ordinarily drift away by then, but she was determined to make the match. It was just a matter of the right approach. She gently nudged her husband again. This time, he caught the hint.

"So, Robert, have you thought about settling down with a woman? Wouldn't hurt to have more helping hands on the farm."

That earned an arched eyebrow from the man. "A woman, you say?"

"I haven't been happier since Amelia came. She's good company and a good worker. Nice with the kids, too. Things have been going so well, I thought you might want to give it a try."

Amelia saw her opportunity and took it.

"I'm happy here, too. Any woman with a strong back and good morals would make a fine wife, don't you think?" she asked.

Robert gave her a strange look. Amelia was afraid he wasn't interested, but she kept trying.

"You see, a dear friend of mine is looking to come out West, and I thought she would be the perfect wife for you."

Robert's brow arched, and he continued to eat his food quietly.

"Well, what do you think?" she asked.

Her anxiety was reaching its peak when her husband again intervened.

"This might be a bit much to take in. Amelia is set on having some female companionship, and she thought it'd be a good idea. Still, I think we might be pushing a little, Robert? Should just let you ponder it."

Robert nodded his head and wiped his mouth on the napkin Amelia had set out. He didn't say a word.

With that, Joseph finished his plate and stood. "I think it's time I help you with the dishes, my dear."

Amelia wasn't happy with the way her suggestion was received, but she did appreciate her husband's help, so the two of them left the table with the children to start the cleanup. She looked back to see Robert staring ahead and saying nothing. She wondered what he could be thinking, but she did notice a little gleam in his eye.

Robert got on his horse and headed home. He thought about what Amelia and Joseph had said and realized there might be something to this Mail Order Bride business. It wasn't like the girl was a complete stranger—since Amelia knew her, and the thought of having someone to take care of the house and help with farm work sounded like a good idea.

Not to mention the pleasure of her company come evening time.

He patted Angus's neck and said, "What do you think? Would ya like to have some feminine touches to the ol' farmstead?"

Angus snorted and continued down the path to home.

"Hmm… that's what I thought. You think I should give it a try, don't ya? Well, I'll look into it tomorrow."

Robert was up before the sun. He put on his dusty clothes and muddy boots and headed outside into the summer sunshine. There was no point in starting off with clean clothes when they'd just get dirty again, he thought, but he did scrape the muck off his boots at the threshold of his front door. He was going to visit the neighbors, after all.

Angus knew the way, and that gave Robert a chance to think some more about finding a wife. Robert wasn't much of a talker, save conversing with Angus, but the horse was a great listener. As the two passed by fields of golden wheat, Robert asked him for advice.

"Angus," he said, "it's been just the two of us since you was a foal. Of course, I've got plenty of other animals, but you and me are family."

The horse nodded his head in rhythm with his gait and continued down the road.

Robert patted Angus' head and continued: "Here's the thing... I'm tired. Tired of doing everything on my own, present company excepted, of course. As you know, we're headn' to the Spencers' for a visit. That Amelia's gonna try n' push me to get married, and I'm startin' to think it's a good idea. That don't mean I don't care for you, ya know. Just want to make that clear."

Angus flicked his ears.

"Glad we came to an agreement," Robert said. "Wouldn't wanna to hurt your feelings none."

When Robert arrived, Amelia came out to greet him while the children played outside. Robert could tell she was excited – maybe too excited for his taste – and she led him inside to the front room. It was a nice home for a farmstead; it had glass windows, wooden floors, and even flowered paper on the walls. Robert didn't usually notice such details, and he sat on an uncomfortable chair "all the way from Boston" and let her fuss over him.

"Want some coffee?" she asked.

He loved coffee, but based on what she made for church dinners, he wasn't too excited. Her coffee was weak, and he thought of it as "dehorned bellywash," but he would never say so in polite company. Instead, he put on a brave face and nodded. Just as he was about to take his first swig, Joseph came in and greeted him.

"Hey, Robert. Good to see ya."

"Indeed, it is good to see you," Amelia added. "Have you thought about our discussion yesterday?"

Robert took a drink and suppressed a wince.

"I have. I'm still not too sure, but it could be good for the farm. Love to have more help."

"The farmhands not keepin' up with the crops this year?" asked Joseph.

"Naw, they're fine, but someone to keep house and feed us'd be good."

Amelia blushed. Robert looked over at her and wondered what he had said to upset her. Women were hard to figure out, he thought.

"Surely you're looking for more than another worker," she said.

"Hadn't given it much thought, but I reckon so. Might be nice to have some company, though I'm not much of a people person."

"Why don't I send her a letter with your photograph. You do have one, don't you?" asked Amelia.

"I do, but it's awful old. Ya don't think it'd scare her off?"

"Mr. Robert Davenport, you're a decent, handsome man."

It was Robert's turn to blush. No one had said a word about his appearance before, and she had no reason to lie, so it must have been true, at least a little bit.

Joseph intervened, "I'm no judge, but I trust my wife. Who knows? This whole thing could be good for ya."

"Just say the word, and I'll send the letter," said Amelia.

Robert steeled his courage and said, "Fine."

By the time Robert arrived home, he was worn out. The one thing he knew to perk him up was working the fields with his men, so that was what he did.

CHAPTER 9

It had been two weeks, and Jenny had heard nothing from Montana. Did she have the wrong address? Was her friend too busy to respond? Did the mail get waylaid? A dozen horrible scenarios passed through her mind, and it gave her a headache. Finally, she calmed down and began to lecture herself. Borrowing trouble wasn't practical, and it was out of character for her. Instead of worrying, she needed to do something about it.

It was time for the mail to arrive, and Jenny assumed her usual hiding spot. Since she'd had so much experience, her timing was impeccable; it was just a matter of patience. Mr. Blake, the butler, had no idea what was going on, of that she was sure, so she had become relaxed with the ritual. While she tried to keep her spirits up, she was sure this was just another day, and she would likely be disappointed again.

Just when she headed toward the letter pile, Mildred came from around the corner and rushed ahead of her. As luck would have it, the letter Jenny had been waiting for was sitting on top, but Mildred grabbed it before Jenny could.

"What are you doing?" Jenny hissed. "That letter is for me. You have no right to…"

"I'm tired of secrets, miss," Mildred replied.

Jenny tried to snatch the letter from Mildred's hands, but the maid was already heading down the hall toward Miss Hooper's office. Jenny was horrified; Miss Hooper was the last person who should know about her correspondence. While Jenny had suspected Mildred could make trouble for her, it was still surprising to her. They'd spent so much time together; did it really mean nothing?

As they raced across the manor, Mildred's feet were making a terrible racket, but Jenny knew better. As servants, they should not be seen or heard while the family was present. To make matters worse, Mildred's clattering attracted the attention of Mrs. Thompson, the lady of the house. Jenny's temples were throbbing with a sudden headache.

Mildred wasn't watching where she was going, and she ran right into Mrs. Thompson, toppling her. The lady wasn't used to such things and didn't know what to say; her beautiful hat was askew, and her neatly coifed hair was awry. She sat on the floor, stunned. Within moments, the butler rushed over and helped her up, but he seemed as flustered as the poor lady of the house. He did his best to put her back together, save for her hair; that was the lady's maid's job.

Jenny stood perfectly still and waited for the storm to hit. Once things were in order and settled down, it would be her turn to be scrutinized. Time slowed to a halt as she prayed the letter contained good news that would counteract her certain dismissal from the only home she'd ever known. She felt queasy and the world closed in on her, blanketing her senses. She felt faint and feared she'd topple over just as the lady of the house had.

When Jenny came to, she was in her bedroom, but she wasn't alone. Roy stood in the doorway, watching over her. He couldn't come inside her room, of course, but there he stood. He was pale, and his eyes were watery.

"Jenny, you okay? You … you hit the floor."

"What… what happened?"

"You fainted, and then Mr. Blake helped you up to your room. It was quite a mess. Mildred is with the mistress now, and I don't know what will happen to her."

"To her?"

"Obviously. She ran across the house like a train and twice as loud, not to mention running into Mrs. Thompson herself. What a strange thing for her to do."

"Roy, something else is wrong. What is it?" Jenny asked with trepidation.

Roy shifted his weight from one foot to the other.

"Jenny, I know about the letter," he said.

"What?"

"Mildred opened the letter and tried to give it to Mrs. Thompson, but there was so much excitement about the incident and you fainting that it was forgotten and lay on the floor. I figured it was best if I took it before the others saw."

"You read it, didn't you?"

Roy looked down and lowered his voice. "I did."

"What did it say? I'd like to have it, since it's mine."

"It's on your desk. I'll leave you be now."

As he turned to go, Jenny stopped him. She'd never seen him so forlorn, not even when she turned down his proposal.

"Please stay," she pleaded. "I can explain."

"You need your rest," he replied and walked away.

~

The letter. It was the thing she'd waited for, worried about, and dreaded all at once. What did it say that made Roy so sad? She sat up and was dizzy immediately, but she was determined. She went to her desk and read the letter.

Dearest Jenny,

I received your letter, and I have wonderful news. I've found a good, strong man who is

interested. His name is Robert Davenport, and I've enclosed a photograph for you to see. He's a wheat farmer and while his cabin isn't fancy, it's comfortable and warm in the winter. You'll love it here. The air is clean, the mountains are beautiful, and the people are kind. Please say you'll come. I can't wait to show you Montana.

Your friend,

Amelia

Jenny held the photograph in her trembling hands and looked at Robert's face. He was handsome, that was for sure, and he had kind eyes and a full head of curly hair. Somewhere deep inside, she knew it was meant to be. She would go to Montana and be his bride.

Then it dawned on her; of course, Roy was upset. They had never been apart more than a day, and that was when he'd been kicked by one of the horses. In all the excitement, she'd forgotten him. How could she help him understand? Even though she'd turned him down, after all, she still loved him like a brother. She would need to think on it.

Jenny's rest was short-lived; she was a servant after all, and supper wouldn't prepare itself. In fact, she now faced twice the work since Mildred wouldn't be there. Then there were the scullery maids. How much did Mildred tell them? How much did they know? Jenny was sure to pick up on their gossip, and that would help her gauge how much trouble lay ahead for her.

When she reached the kitchen, the maids looked up from their work to stare at her. It was worse than she thought; they were afraid. Jenny knew what to do. It was time to speak with Mrs. Thompson. She took off her apron, straightened her hair, washed her face, and gave the maids instructions for dinner. Then, she made her way to the parlor.

There was Mrs. Thompson, still shaken from that morning's collision with Mildred. She was sitting in her favorite chair, looking out the window.

"Mrs. Thompson? Do you have a moment?"

Mrs. Thompson turned to look at her.

"Yes, Jenny, what is it? Is it about earlier today? Why were you chasing Mildred? She claimed there was some secret nonsense, but I trust you."

Jenny cleared her throat and dug her nails into her hands. It was an old trick she learned to keep herself from becoming too emotional.

"Well, about today…"

"Yes?"

Jenny closed her eyes and proceeded. This would be harder than she thought.

"The truth is, I've found someone to marry."

"Is it the Roy fellow? He's always been fond of you."

"Umm, no, ma'am. It's someone else. Someone from Montana. I expect you'll want me to vacate my position and clear out my things."

Mrs. Thompson twisted the emerald ring on her left index finger. She did this whenever she was uncomfortable.

"I'm sorry to hear it, truly I am," she said. "I must say I'm shocked you chose someone on the other side of the country to wed instead of our dear stable hand, but you are old enough to make your own decisions. I've always liked you, Jenny, so I will give you time to make arrangements before you go. You deserve that much."

"Oh, ma'am, thank you," Jenny said with feeling. "I've always known you to be generous, and I couldn't be more grateful."

"I'll send a good reference with you, too. One never knows when one might need it. Take care, Jenny. I pray this groom of yours is all you hope for. You may go now."

It was a lovely summer morning. This was the day Jenny's dreams would come true; she was finally leaving the manor. She had already said her goodbyes to the other servants, save Roy. That meant the hardest part was yet to come.

Ordinarily, Roy didn't drive the carriage, as his duties were confined to the stables, but Mrs. Thompson herself gave him permission to drive Jenny to the train station. He didn't look at her as he helped her enter the carriage and closed the door. Instead, he focused on the horses. Once the carriage began moving, sadness interrupted her excitement for a new adventure.

The trip wouldn't take long. Jenny was trying to think of what to say to her dear childhood friend. How could she let him go without hurting him even more? Should she ask him to write, or would that be inappropriate? So many questions shot through her mind as the carriage rode on.

They arrived. She had just thirty minutes until the train left, so she couldn't dawdle, but she mustn't rush off too soon either. Roy opened the carriage door for her and led her by the hand to the sidewalk. His face was ashen, and his eyes were pained. It was hard for her to see him like that, but she had to make him understand why she was doing this.

"Roy, dear, please don't be sad."

"Why are you leaving? Everything you've known and all the people who love you are here. Are you really going to marry a man you don't know? Is it that bad here? Am I that unbearable?"

Jenny reached up and touched his cheek softly. She gave him a sad smile and said, "Oh, Roy, you're the reason why it's so hard to go. I do care for you, but I need this new adventure. I need to try life without being a servant."

Tears welled in his eyes. "You'll be late for your train, Jenny. I suppose it's time for you to go."

She began to cry. Why didn't it feel as good as she imagined it would? Was she making the right decision?

"I'll never forget you," she whispered.

Before she could say another word, Roy wrapped his arms around her and squeezed her tightly. He abruptly let her go and didn't say another word as he waved goodbye. Jenny got on her train, settled in, and watched him until he was out of sight.

CHAPTER 10

Robert fidgeted with his collar. He hated this kind of shirt; they were tight, hot, and uncomfortable. Still, Amelia had insisted he wear it to look like a gentleman. He reluctantly agreed, but now he regretted it.

"When's the stagecoach due again?" he asked.

"Robert, you know it's due any minute now. Stop fussing. You need to make a good impression."

He tried to hold still, but it felt like he was a boy again at Christmas. Every year, his parents would force him to dress up in his itchy Sunday best clothes and sit still, "like a good boy." He shuddered and wondered if he'd have to do this all the time now.

There it was – the stagecoach. He knew his future bride had taken the train for the first part of her journey but had to change to a stagecoach for the last bit. Any minute now, she would walk out of the coach and into his life, like it or not. Had he made a good decision? Was this going to work out? Would she be a decent helper on the farm and keep up the house, or would she be lazy? His head swarmed with questions as the stagecoach pulled to a stop, billowing dust everywhere. Here she was.

Jenny stepped down onto solid ground. It had been too long since she hadn't been in motion, as the trip took longer than she thought it would. The stagecoach portion had been even more uncomfortable than the train. She felt shaky and a little nauseated, not just from the trip, but from facing her dream head-on.

When she got her bearings, she saw her dear friend, Amelia, standing with a tall, good-looking man and two children. There he was, Robert Davenport. Sure enough, he was as handsome as his picture, and now that she saw him in color, she noticed his thick, curly hair was a handsome auburn – not too red and not too dark. His eyes were brilliant blue, and his face was pink from both the sun and his blushing. Could he be as nervous as she was? And who were the children?

"Hello, Miss Jansen… err Jenny, I'm Robert. This here's… well, you know Mrs. Henderson…err Amelia."

Jenny and Amelia gave each other a quick hug. Amelia introduced her to her husband's two children.

"So glad to know you," Jenny murmured.

Robert shuffled his boot in the dirt and fidgeted with his collar. Amelia gave him a not-so-gentle jab in the ribs and whispered in his ear, and then Robert stood still without squirming. Amelia gave Jenny another hug. It was enough to leave Jenny breathless, but she didn't mind. She was here in Montana with her good friend and her future husband.

"Let me get your things," said Robert.

Jenny nodded, and he hoisted her trunk into his wagon.

"Amelia and Joseph thought it'd be best if you stayed with them until the weddin'. What do ya think of that? Good idea, keeping your reputation intact, if you ask me," said Robert.

"Yes, yes," Jenny said, suddenly feeling overwhelmed and not a little discombobulated. "It'll be nice to catch up with Amelia."

"And I can't wait for you to meet Joseph. He's a good man, just like Robert. I'm taking my wagon back to our house. You'll go with Robert."

Jenny turned to smile at Robert, but he was already in his wagon, ready to go. She was shocked to see he wasn't going to help her up, but she didn't let herself get upset about it. Perhaps that was the way they did things here.

As she and Robert pulled way, Amelia gathered up the children and called out, "Let's go to my house. I'll make some coffee, and we can gab for as long as we want. It'll give you time to get to know Bartholomew and Ruby, too."

"All right, Amelia. Sounds good," Jenny agreed.

The road through town was bumpy and uneven, and Robert's wagon was not like the carriages she was used to. She was bounced around the rough, wooden seat so often that she thought she'd be thrown off. In the meantime, she'd hoped to get to know Robert a little more.

Unfortunately, at least a half an hour passed before Robert said anything, and Jenny wasn't sure what to think of that. Didn't he like her? Did he still want her? Had she done something wrong? A thousand questions shot through her mind as she sat beside him. This was going to be harder than she thought.

"Robert," she began, "this is beautiful country. I've never seen mountains so tall. And is that snow on top? In summer?"

Robert shifted in his seat. An uncomfortable number of seconds went by before he responded.

"Hmm… yeah, it's pretty, I 's'pose."

Another few agonizing moments passed. The awkwardness was painful for Jenny; she'd never met someone who said so little. Compelled to fill the silence, she tried again.

"Is your farm very far?"

"Not far, no."

"How big is it? What do you grow? Do you have animals?"

Robert shifted in his seat once again. "Well, it's fairly good-sized. Grow wheat, mostly. Got plenty of animals, I reckon."

As far as Jenny was concerned, reaching her friend's house couldn't come soon enough. This was awful. Still, she knew there should be some way to connect with him. She just hadn't found it yet.

When they finally pulled up to Amelia's and Joseph's house, Jenny was wide-eyed. The house seemed small and crude to her, but she had lived in a mansion all her life. Things were bound to be different here.

Robert made no attempt to help her out of the wagon, so Joseph stepped in and did it instead. Robert didn't seem to notice his lack of etiquette, and no one said anything. Perhaps he didn't know any better, Jenny thought. She pushed her reservations aside and gave Amelia another big hug.

"And this here is Joseph," Amelia said proudly.

"Glad to know you," Joseph said with a smile.

"I can't wait to show you inside," said Amelia. "You'll love it here. I just know it. I can't wait to introduce you to the rest of the town."

Jenny raised her eyebrow and asked, "The whole town? Won't that take a long time?"

"Oh, my dear friend, this ain't Boston. There aren't more than a couple dozen families here. You should know, too, that you and I are just about the only women who live here."

Jenny's eyes grew wide.

"That's right. We really are on the frontier, you know, and now we can hold ladies' meetings and activities. Oh, I can't wait."

Everyone went inside and sat down. To Jenny's surprise, Robert chose to sit next to Joseph, rather than her. Not surprisingly, he didn't say a word. Amelia picked up on the tension in the room and cleared her throat.

"Could I interest you all in some coffee? It'll just take a moment."

Robert's face contorted ever so slightly at the mention of coffee. For the life of her, Jenny had no idea why. In the meantime, she waited for her friend and sat very still, wanting to see if either of the men would say a word. Fortunately, Joseph broke the silence.

"Robert, I heard your ox took lame, is that right?" he asked.

"For a bit, but I took care of it."

"Hmm…" Joseph said. "Perhaps you could tell us what happened?"

Amelia came back in the room and nudged Joseph with her foot.

"Perhaps that's not a conversation my friend would like to hear."

"No, it's all right. I'm used to stories about the horses in our stables. Roy used to…" she trailed off.

"Roy? How's that boy doing?"

Jenny's heart started to quaver, but she couldn't let it show.

"He's fine, I suppose. He's the new stable master now."

"Ah, well ain't that nice?" said Amelia.

Amelia walked back into the kitchen and poured everyone a cup of coffee. Jenny took her cup and tried a sip. While she didn't let it show on her face, she thought Amelia's coffee was the worst she'd ever had. It was so weak it tasted like hot water and a little grit. She would have to teach her how to make it properly.

Just then, Bartholomew burst through the front door. Ruby followed close behind, crying.

"My goodness, what happened?" asked Amelia.

"My… my chicken. I can't find her," Ruby cried.

Bartholomew put his arm over the little girl's shoulder.

"I looked, but I didn't see nothin'. Could be a coyote got her."

The thought of her precious chicken being harmed sent Ruby into new, more intense sobs. Amelia wiped the tears off Ruby's cheeks and kissed her forehead.

"Sweet Amelia, I separated her because the other hens were pecking her too much. I think it's because she's so much smaller. I put her in the barn. You'll see her right off. She's next to where we keep the mare. After we're finished visiting, I'll show you where she is. Or you could go visit her right now."

Ruby sniffed hard and then a lovely smile broke out over her face. "Thank you, Auntie."

Then, just as soon as they had entered, the children left, and the house seemed strangely quiet. Jenny's heart went out to the girl, and she couldn't help but smile at how her friend handled the situation.

"They call you auntie?" she asked.

"Yes, mama just didn't seem right."

"I told her it would be fine, but Amelia's awful sensitive about keepin' the kids happy," added Joseph.

Soon, the conversation turned again to farming. A few hours later, Jenny knew little more about Robert than when they first met. Amelia had said he didn't talk much, but it was surprising to her just how much it was true.

Robert fidgeted with his collar again before standing. His eyes never left the floor as he said, "Time I left. Good to see ya'll. Meet ya at the church for the weddin', Jenny."

"Won't I see you until then?" Jenny asked.

"Got work at the farm. Gettin' things ready for harvest next month. See you Saturday."

With that, he stood up, shook Joseph's hand, and made his way out the door. Jenny watched him go. Confusion filled her; didn't he want to learn more about her? Didn't he care? Amelia sensed her unease and gave her a hug.

"It'll be all right. Like I said, he's not much of a talker," she said.

"But why doesn't he want to see me before the wedding?"

"The menfolk here care about their fields and little else." Amelia laughed. "Mine's a little better about it unless someone brings up the topic. Don't worry—he'll come around."

It was Saturday, the day of the wedding. Jenny, Amelia, the children, and Joseph were already at the church, and the reverend was sitting patiently beside the altar. There, in a small room next to the door, Amelia fussed over Jenny's hair, trying to make it perfect.

"You're so lovely, Jenny. I think this style will suit you… or maybe not. Would you like to try more ribbons?"

Jenny was pensive.

"Any sign of Robert?" she asked. "The wedding should start soon. Do you think he remembered?"

Had he changed his mind? Then what would she do? Where would she go? Amelia could see the worry on her face and tried to cheer her up.

"Why wouldn't he remember? He's a lucky man, you know. Maybe he's running behind. It isn't as easy to get around out here."

"Maybe," Jenny said.

She wasn't convinced, but she rallied her courage and finished preparing. Her dress was just her Sunday best since she only had two other dresses, and they weren't good enough to be married in. She held a small bouquet of wildflowers Ruby had picked for her. They were just starting to wilt, and they reminded her of Roy, but she knew that was inappropriate. She was marrying someone else, after all.

Just when Jenny had given up hope, Robert walked in the door. He too had his Sunday best on, and she could tell he'd bathed for the occasion. That made her happy enough, so she walked down the aisle to meet him. There was no music and no crowd; it was just Amelia and Joseph, functioning as witnesses and the children, who were on their best behavior.

As Jenny and Robert exchanged vows, she tried to maintain eye contact, but he was too nervous to hold her gaze. This wedding was not going the way she thought. She had never wanted a big fancy ceremony, but a little romance wouldn't hurt.

The ceremony concluded, and it was time for Robert to "kiss the bride." She held her breath and leaned in. Unfortunately, he didn't lean in, and she felt foolish. Her eyes brimmed with tears, and then he kissed her on the cheek. That was something, she thought, but it wasn't romantic in the least.

The wagon ride to Robert's homestead was as awkward as the first time they rode together. He focused on the horse and didn't say anything. By this time, Jenny understood silence was going to be a common occurrence, but she tried to start a conversation anyway.

"Well, we're officially married now," she said.

"Yep," he relied.

"I'd like to get to know you, Robert. We're going to spend our lives together, after all."

Robert grunted and kept looking down the road.

"There's the farm," he said. "I'll show you around."

She looked around at if for the first time. Just as in her dream, the wind blew softly through the swaying wheat fields, creating a river-like sound. The crops were golden, and the sun was shining over the horizon. Impossibly large mountains with snowy caps and jagged edges framed the valley and gave a sense of protection.

Just beyond the fields to her left, a humble cabin stood, but there were no children or flowers, just dirt. At least some of her dream was coming true, she thought. It took her a while to get out of the wagon because her dress caught on a jagged edge of the seat, and by the time her feet were on the ground, Robert was halfway to the front door, carrying her trunk. She sighed and followed him in.

The cabin wasn't as nice as Amelia's; there were a couple of glass windows, but they were small and didn't let much light in. The floors were dirt, and the walls were made of mud daub and sawn logs. She was used to grand windows and decorations, but she would have to adjust. This was her life now.

"Here's where we sleep," he said and pointed to the only other room in the house. "Trunk's in there."

She wasted no time in unpacking her things. She didn't own much, but having some familiar things around would make her feel better. As she unpacked, she noticed he wasn't good at laundering his clothes; well, she could take care of that from now on. She finished and walked out to the main room where the kitchen was located. A fly buzzed about some of the dirty plates he had stacked on the counter. She was strangely happy about it; cleaning would give her something to do, after all.

"You all right? Need anything? If not, I'll see ya later," said Robert. "Gotta finish the chores. Maybe you could have supper ready."

"All right, but…"

Jenny's sentence was interrupted by the door closing behind Robert. Instead of giving into her growing disappointment, she focused on prayer. As she prayed, she found comfort and got busy straightening, cleaning, and cooking.

There wasn't much to choose from for Jenny to make a supper, but her years of experience lent her enough skills to make up for it. She fried up the last of his bacon and added the grease to a little batch of cornbread, for the pork flavor would make the cornbread much tastier. There wasn't much coffee left, but she knew how to stretch it without sacrificing too much taste.

While the cornbread was baking, she cleaned up the kitchen, dusted and tidied the furniture, and sorted the dirty clothes. She decided she would wash them along with the sheets tomorrow. By the time Robert returned, the cabin was almost unrecognizable.

His eyes grew wide.

"Looks great, Jenny. Kitchen's clean and it smells good. What's for supper?"

It was the most she'd heard him speak. She reveled in her success; perhaps this could

work out after all. She just needed to work hard and be helpful. Supper was already on the table, so they sat down, and he began to eat right away. He did have some table manners, but she could tell he was hungry. After he'd eaten half his cornbread, he reached for the coffee. There was the same contorted expression she had seen at Amelia's. Could it be that he just didn't like coffee? Then again, she thought, Amelia's coffee was awful.

After a tentative sip, Robert's eyes brightened, and he smiled. It was the first time she'd seen him smile, and it was very flattering to his face. Dimples formed in his cheeks as he took another drink.

"Great coffee. Was afraid it'd be like Amelia's. I like that woman fine, but her coffee is awful."

"You're welcome, and I agree."

She chuckled and smiled. There was a soft side to him, perhaps. She just needed to find a way to bring it out. Jenny resolved to use her cooking skills to warm both his stomach and his heart.

CHAPTER 11

The next day, Jenny woke up in confusion. Nothing had happened the night before, despite it being their wedding night. They'd each slept on their own side of the bed, and that was that. When Jenny saw Amelia again, she'd ask about it. It would be painfully embarrassing, but she felt the need to talk to someone about it.

Robert was already up and out in the fields, so after a bite to eat, Jenny started in on the washing. Laundry was backbreaking work, but she wasn't afraid to use some muscle. It took a long time to get the baked-on dirt out of his pants, socks, and long johns, but by the time she was finished, not a spot remained. Her own dusty clothes were clean as well.

She revamped his clothesline to be sturdier so it would hold more weight and hung their clothes out to dry. Before she started on the sheets, however, she needed to get the larder in order. That meant buying supplies.

Jenny hadn't driven a wagon before, so she picked her way through the fields to find Robert. There he was, working with his farmhands. Fall would be here soon, and it would be time to harvest.

"Robert, could you take me to town? I don't know how to drive a wagon," she said.

He looked up from his work and wiped his sweaty brow.

"Too busy to take you. One of my boys can. Gotta teach you soon, so you can do it yerself."

He called over a scrawny boy with a straw hat and sent him out with Jenny. She was disappointed that he'd delegated the job to someone else, but she also knew he had work to do. It was just that back in Boston, if she ever needed anything, Roy would stop what he was doing to help. But that was then, and now she was in Montana, her dream place. She had to stop making comparisons.

When she and the boy returned home from the general store, it was already time to prepare a meal. She had assumed everyone had already eaten breakfast due to the late hour. But she discovered to her chagrin, that they had been waiting on her. Not surprisingly, the boys were hungry, so she whipped up some quick eggs and potatoes and promised to do better next time. The laundry would have to wait until later in the day from now on, she decided.

Going to the barn, Robert checked on Angus. The horse was munching happily on his hay when Robert came in. He flicked his ears forward and flapped a lip up in greeting, and Robert gave him a few pats on the neck.

"Angus, she's a hard worker. Makes good food, too. I'm thinkin' this was a good idea, don't you?"

The horse whinnied.

"Hmm… you don't think so? You should meet her. Think you might like her."

Robert felt happy, now that the house was clean, and he didn't have to cook anymore. Doing double duty had been especially tiring, but he didn't realize it until the weight was lifted.

As he headed back to the house, he decided to introduce Angus to Jenny later that day. For now, it was time to eat. He and the boys sat around his large wooden table with mismatched chairs while Jenny served them. It wasn't as much food as he'd hoped, but what they did have was delicious.

"I hope you enjoyed it," said Jenny after clearing the dishes. "I've got more ideas for future meals."

The farmhands heaped praise on her while Robert sat back and tried to think of something to say. It was hard for him to speak with anyone besides Angus, let alone a woman. He feared she wouldn't be happy here, especially since he didn't say much, but he would do his best. From what he'd seen, she was a good woman and on her way to being a good wife, and he wanted to express that to her. The problem was he had no idea how.

"Great food," Robert said. He traced lines across the table with his finger. "Real good. Thanks," he mumbled.

Hopefully that was enough for her to know he cared, Robert thought. It was hard to say, but he'd keep trying. The strain was weighing on him, and it was time to get back to work, so he stood and walked toward the door.

"I'll show you the garden tomorrow," he said.

She looked puzzled. "The garden?"

"Later," he replied. "Got to go now. C'mon boys."

The days and weeks went by too quickly, and then it was the official start of the harvest. Summer had made its exit, and fall blew in with cool winds and falling leaves. That morning,

Jenny was up before Robert and started working on breakfast. She had never repeated her first mistake of offering breakfast too late. The boys worked too hard for that, and they were used to starting the day earlier than her previous employers.

As she finished stirring the last dish, she heard Robert stirring in the bedroom, so she poured a cup of coffee for him and set it down at the table.

"Mornin'," said Robert.

He rubbed his eyes with his calloused hands. Jenny noticed he was working up a smile, and she thought it made him look like a mischievous puppy.

It warmed her heart, and she replied, "Did you have a good night's sleep? I made you some coffee. It's on the table."

He didn't grimace anymore when she served coffee, so she assumed he was happy with her brew. Though neither of them said much, she felt a sense of warmth from him that morning, and it surprised her. Perhaps there was potential for some romance after all. Jenny appreciated his work ethic and the way he treated the workers, but she also wanted some affection, and she hoped that would come naturally.

"Gonna be a long day," he said, breaking the silence. "How's the garden comin' along?"

"I did everything you told me to, and the plants are healthy and growing and about ready to harvest."

"Good to hear. Say, d'ya know Amelia and Joseph are stoppin' by with the little ones?"

"Are they?" she asked, smiling.

She enjoyed their visits, even though she was inexperienced with children. All her life, she'd only worked with other servants, never children. She tried to make friends with them, and felt she was making some progress.

"I'll get some more coffee ready," she said.

There was a knock at the door, and all four of the Spencers came in. Bartholomew had a wooden whistle in hand, ready to make a racket, while Ruby clung to Amelia's skirt. Amelia reached over and gave Jenny a big hug.

"I'm so glad you agreed. It would be too long a trip for the children to come with us," said Amelia.

What was this? Jenny's pulse quickened. Robert had said nothing about looking after children. She had no idea what to do, and a sense of panic began to wash over her. Blood rushed to her cheeks, and Amelia noticed something wasn't quite right.

"Robert did tell you about watching the children, right?" she asked.

"Um… of course. We'll give it our best try," Jenny replied.

It was Amelia's turn to blush. "Oh, my dear, I'm so sorry. If you like, we could take the children…"

"No, it's fine Amelia. I'll find something fun for us to do."

"That's wonderful. It's just a couple days. You're such a good sport. Just remember that they have naps in the early afternoon; otherwise, they can be quite grumpy."

"I'm not grumpy," protested Bartholomew. "I'm great. I got a whistle, see? I'm good at blowin' it, too."

The little boy took a deep breath and blew as hard as he could. The sound coming out of that whittled wooden whistle took Jenny's breath away. Never in her life had she heard something so loud and unpleasant.

"Don't worry, Jenny. I'll take it with me," said Amelia.

"No. No, I want my whistle," cried Bartholomew.

This was not going well, and it made Jenny even more uncomfortable. But she was going to do her best. "Bartholomew, please calm yourself. You may not have your whistle, but I have other things you can do, you'll see. Besides, Ruby isn't crying. You don't want to upset her, do you?"

The little boy contemplated what she said, and then handed the whistle to Jenny.

"I reckon I don't need it," he said. "I've gotta show Ruby 'round. Got stuff to do."

With that, Jenny smiled and Amelia patted Bartholomew's head and gave both children a kiss.

"Oh Jenny, I almost forgot. I brought a thank you gift for helping us out. I know how much you love flowers, so I brought a pot of them for your front step. I can't wait to show you. Come with me."

There, in their wagon, was the flowerpot from her dreams. Daisies crowded over the top and showed their yellow faces up to the sun. Jenny kept a calm exterior, but it thrilled her. Another piece of her dream was coming true.

She looked over her shoulder and saw the children already at play. Ruby was chasing her brother, and they were having fun playing tag. The only thing missing was the stranger with his arm about her waist. Oh, to have a gentle touch, a gentle kiss, a gentle word. She held back her tears and watched the children.

"Time we headed out," said Joseph. "Thanks again. It should be a quick trip. I am meeting with the grange over in Locksmith. I'm one of the officers. After the meetings, we'll be back. You kids behave, ya hear?"

"Yes, Papa," both children answered.

Jenny hoped beyond hope they meant it.

CHAPTER 12

The harvest was nearly underway. It was time to get out the equipment, give out orders, and get to work. It was Robert's favorite time of year, but something wasn't right. The air was just a little too still, and the animals were too quiet.

He glanced around, worried. And then he saw it. There, on the horizon, was a vast black cloud. It was moving quickly and headed straight for them. Robert knew exactly what it was, and his heart skipped a beat.

"Locusts! We've got locusts!" Robert hollered, panicked.

Jenny had just finished tucking the children in bed for a nap when the sky grew dark. It struck her as odd, considering it was midday. There hadn't been any clouds in the sky or dust on the horizon, so she wondered what it could be.

She walked over to the door and looked outside but saw nothing unusual. Still the darkness seemed to be thickening. She stepped outside and walked around to the back of the house. Her breath caught. A massive black cloud was heading their way. Could a storm move that quickly? Jenny saw Robert out in the field, shouting and pointing. The rest of his men were also shouting.

Jenny frowned. Something was very wrong. She picked up her skirts and ran out through the wheat field to her husband. The closer she got, the bigger the cloud became. It looked like a dust storm, only darker, and it began to roar. Jenny shivered though it wasn't cold.

"Robert! Robert, what's happening?" she shouted over the growing noise.

"Get the animals in the barn now!" Robert yelled to his men. "Quick! Round them up."

The men tore off, heading toward the corrals and then the barn. The noise of the cloud and the hollering and the animals reached fever pitch as they herded the oxen, the pigs, and the chickens into the barn and closed the door.

Jenny watched them in horror. What could be so dangerous that made them so scared? She hadn't seen fear like that on

Robert's face since she met him. He was a strong, hard-working man, and nothing ever changed his calm exterior.

There was pure panic on his face.

"Angus! Angus is out in the pasture. You there, you men start digging the trenches. We'll try to smoke them out. Get the fire ready! We've got to keep them locusts from devouring the crops."

Locusts! Jenny had heard of them.

Robert grabbed her arm. "Get inside with the children. The locusts—they'll eat everything in their path. Now go."

"The children are sleeping. What can I do to help?"

"Block the windows and cracks in the wall with anything you can find!"

She raced back to the house, through her garden. Tears filled her eyes as she thought about the locusts devouring everything she'd worked so hard to grow. The whirr of the insects grew to a deafening pitch.

The children! If they awoke, they'd be frightened. She flew into the house, slamming the door behind her. She heard the resounding pings against the window. The locusts were upon them now.

Robert ran blindly to the pasture in a panic. Where was Angus? Had they already taken him? The locusts rained down on his hat and in his face, making it difficult to see.

"Angus! Angus! Come here, boy."

There, in the far corner of the pasture, he made out Angus running at a full gallop, his eyes white with panic. Robert held up his hands in a calming gesture. Angus trembled before him.

"Here boy, good boy! It's all right. I got ya! I got ya," he yelled over the roar of insects.

He jumped on and rode Angus to the barn as fast as he could. The boys had already secured the barn. Robert slid down and worked to shove the door aside. He blinked against the insects. The door was stuck.

Just then, Jenny ran out to him. What was she doing?

"Robert! Robert, I can help. Tell me what to do."

Together they shoved against the door, finally loosing it so that it opened. Angus ran in. Insects swarmed inside, too, but they got it shut quickly enough to avoid the worst. By now, the sky was so thick with locusts, it was hard to see. Robert pushed Jenny toward the house.

"Get inside. Stay safe. I… I love you."

Jenny's eyes grew wide. "I love you too. We'll get through this. We'll…"

Her words were drowned out by the raging sound—the sound of millions of insect mouths eating everything in sight. Robert felt a sudden terror at the thought of losing her—losing everything.

He pushed her again toward the house. He prayed for his family, his workers, and his crops. Surely, something would be spared.

By the time Jenny closed the door to their little cabin, the locusts were flying at full force. Dozens were creeping under the door and through the cracks in the walls. She cried out, batting at them with the broom. She prayed for strength and help.

The children had awakened from the noise, and they were screaming. She had no time to comfort them; instead, she showed them how to stuff up the holes where the insects were coming in. In the meantime, she grabbed items of clothing and blankets and tore them into strips for more material. Still the locusts came.

The fear of utter destruction grabbed Jenny as she gathered the children close. They needed cover for protection, so she grabbed the last blanket they owned and pulled it over them. She tucked in all the corners under their feet and held onto the children as the monstrous infestation continued.

Hours seemed to go by and the roar didn't abate. The children shook in her arms, and then suddenly, it all stopped. There was nothing. Dead silence. She pulled the blanket back a bit and saw daylight.

It was over.

Robert looked around the farm. All his crops. All his wheat. Gone. All of it. Just gone as if it had never been.

His chest heaved and his throat ached with tears. Gone.

He was ruined. *They* were ruined.

His men had sheltered in the barn. They stumbled out one at a time. In silence, they took in the carnage. No one spoke. They avoided looking at each other. They all knew what this meant.

No crops—no money.

Robert would lose his workers. He couldn't pay them. He couldn't feed them.

He was ruined.

He sucked in his breath, fighting despair, when he heard a whinny. And there was Angus. The horse walked slowly to where he stood and put his nose on Robert's shoulder.

Jenny cautiously pulled off the blanket and looked around. There were still a few locusts beating against the inside window, but the masses were gone. They were safe. She hugged the children so tightly that Bartholomew complained he couldn't breathe, but Ruby tucked her head in and leaned on Jenny.

Jenny told the children to stay put, and she headed out to look for her husband. She spotted him by the barn with his beloved horse. And then she saw the fields and her heart sank. Gone. It was all gone. They had nothing left.

She ran to Robert's side and buried her face in his chest.

"What will we do?" she said, muffled by his flannel shirt.

"I-I'll think of somethin'," he said. "We're gonna make it. We gotta."

They stood together, holding each other up, desperately clinging to one another. When Jenny finally pulled away, Robert wiped the tears from her cheeks. And then, he bent toward her and kissed her. She sucked in her breath and kissed him back, mindless of the workers standing around. And then he took her hand, grasping it as if he'd never let go.

Though her heart was breaking, the touch of his lips and the feel of his hand gave her courage. They would make it, just like he said. They had to.

And then something dawned on her. The garden. Did the garden make it? She pulled away from Robert and ran to the garden patch. Nothing. It was a flat patch of empty dirt. She fell to her knees and frantically started digging, her fingers scraping into the dirt. The root vegetables. The locusts couldn't have gotten to them. Tears streamed down her face as she uprooted radishes and beets.

"Look," she cried to Robert. "Look!"

Robert had followed after her and now stood gazing at her with such intensity that she felt him to her very core. She laughed through her tears and stood up, hurrying to him. She threw herself into his open arms. His warm embrace was all she wanted—all she needed.

The children came out to meet them. Their eyes were wide, but the fear was gone from their faces. Bartholomew glanced around and then his eyes settled on Jenny.

"Can I have my whistle back now?" he asked.

Wind blew softly through the swaying wheat fields, creating a river-like sound. The crops were gone, but the sun was setting over the horizon. Impossibly large mountains with snowy caps and jagged edges framed the valley and gave her a sense of protection.

Just beyond the fields to her left, a humble cabin stood, and young children were playing outside. The cabin was small but tidy, and a flowerpot sat by the door. The flowers were gone too, but Jenny would replant it.

A shadowy figure of a man walked up from behind her and set his arm around her waist.

It was Robert, and he whispered in her ear, "I love you, Jenny. Thank you for being my wife."

Jenny leaned into him and sighed deeply with contentment. "I love you, too, husband. Thank you for marrying me."

The End

Thank you for reading *Jenny's Shy Groom!* Are you wondering **what to read next?** Why not read *Finding Nellie?* **Here's a peek for you:**

"Eleanor Williams. How many times must I call you before you respond? Mr. Owens has been waiting for ten minutes."

The sound of her mother's voice bellowing up the stairs in their direction caused both Nellie and her younger sister Alice to break into giggles. Adelaide Williams prided herself on her gentility and good manners. It wasn't her fault her daughters so frequently provoked her to indecorous volumes.

"She sounds like a farmer calling the pigs to come and eat," Alice whispered, trying to control her laughter.

Nellie shook her head, gradually regaining her own control. "Don't be so disrespectful, Alice, you know what Mother would say if she heard you say such things."

"She wouldn't say anything," Alice said. "She'd yell it."

Nellie's giggles returned in full force, and she turned away from her sister to face the mirror once more, trying to finish the task at hand. She was well aware that Percival Owens was waiting for her downstairs – and he could continue to wait until she was finished putting her hair up in the complicated new style she'd seen so recently in the magazines from Paris.

"I don't know why you bother with that," Alice said from her seat on the bed behind her. Alice was just sixteen and had no beau yet. Nellie could remember that time in her life all too well – it had ended rather quickly, when Percy started inviting himself to dinner. Over the years, they had become friends – he was steady and reliable, as evidenced by the fact that he always showed up on time for their engagements. She, meanwhile – well, she had other things to think about.

"Percy likes it," she told her sister.

"So?" said Alice pragmatically. "You don't really care what Percy likes."

"Alice. That's just downright rude – and presumptuous." She frowned at her sister in the reflection of the mirror.

"Maybe so," said Alice, shrugging, "but that doesn't mean it isn't true."

Nellie's eyes returned to her own reflection, studying it. She knew herself to be a pretty girl – perhaps one of the prettiest in their small town of Middleburg, Virginia. Percy was not the only young man to have taken notice of her, he was simply the most persistent. But he suffered from the same malady that afflicted all the men in Middleburg – they were decent, polite, upstanding, and as boring as afternoon tea with Great-Grandmother Meta.

Visit HERE To Read More!

https://ticahousepublishing.com/mail-order-brides.html

THANKS FOR READING!

If you **love Mail Order Bride Romance**, <u>Visit Here</u>

https://wesrom.subscribemenow.com/

to find out about all <u>**New Susannah Calloway Romance Releases!** **We will let you know as soon as they become available!**</u>

If you enjoyed *Jenny's Shy Groom,* would you kindly take a couple minutes to leave a positive review on Amazon? It only takes a moment, and positive reviews truly make a difference. Thank you so much! I appreciate it!

Turn the page to discover more Mail Order Bride Romances just for you!

ABOUT THE AUTHOR

Susannah has always been intrigued with the Western movement - prairie days, mail-order brides, the gold rush, frontier life! As a writer, she's excited to combine her love of story with her love of all that is Western. Presently, Susannah lives in Wyoming with her hubby and their three amazing children.

www.ticahousepublishing.com
contact@ticahousepublishing.com